#1

THE DARIO QUINCY
ACADEMY OF DANCE

Leaping at
SHADOWS

THE DARIO QUINCY
ACADEMY OF DANCE

#1

Leaping at
SHADOWS

BY MEGAN ATWOOD

MINNEAPOLIS

Darby Creek
A division of Lerner Publishing Group, Inc.
241 First Avenue North
Minneapolis, MN 55401 U.S.A.

Website address: www.lernerbooks.com

Cover and interior photographs © Hans Neleman/Stone/Getty Images (main); © iStockphoto.com/Selahattin BAYRAM (paper background).

Main body text set in Janson Text LT Std 12/17.5.
Typeface provided by Linotype AG.

Library of Congress Cataloging-in-Publication Data

Atwood, Megan.
 Leaping at shadows / by Megan Atwood.
  pages cm. — (The Dario Quincy Academy of Dance ; #1)
  ISBN 978–1–4677–0930–9 (lib. bdg. : alk. paper)
  ISBN 978–1–4677–1627–7 (eBook)
  [1. Dance—Fiction. 2. Haunted places—Fiction. 3. Supernatural—Fiction.] I. Title.
 PZ7.A8952Le 2013
 [Fic]—dc23   2012046156

Manufactured in the United States of America
1 – BP – 7/15/13

To my parents, for their constant support.
And to Patrick, who literally held me up when I
fell down. My love and gratitude to you.

Chapter 1

The building looked like it smelled. Old. Like a grandfather's closet. Or a mortuary.

Madeleine shouldered her bag, straightened her shirt, and touched her necklace. She started up the first step of the massive, ancient-looking building in front of her. For reasons she couldn't understand, looking at the windows along the building, shrouded in darkness, made her shiver. It was morning, after all. Did the sun not shine on this place?

"Hey, what about a hug goodbye, at least?"

Madeleine whirled around and smiled at her mom sheepishly. "Sorry. Of course."

She touched her necklace again—the necklace that had belonged to her grandmother; then her mother; and now, as a going-away present, to Madeleine—and bounded down the stairs to wrap her mom in a hug. The idling station wagon next to them let out a bang and a puff of smoke. Madeleine and her mom jumped and then shared a laugh. When they separated, Madeleine saw tears in her mom's eyes.

Her mom sighed and held Madeleine by the shoulders. "It's just until Christmas, and then you come back. Three months. This is your chance, Madeleine. You're so good—you got in two weeks after the semester started, which I was told several times they never do. Don't mess it up." She winked, then said softly, "My talented, beautiful daughter. I will miss you."

Madeleine laughed and wiped tears from her eyes. Her mother had sacrificed a lot to send Madeleine away, even with the scholarship. "I won't let you down, Mom. I'm going to blow them away!"

Her mom nodded and walked to the driver's-side door. "You better. I wouldn't expect anything less." As she got inside, she called out, "Maybe you should bourrée them away!"

Madeleine giggled and shook her head. That was her mom. Cheesy to the bone. Madeleine's heart hurt as she thought about leaving her for two whole months.

Her mom shifted into drive, and Madeleine watched her pull away, waving like a crazy woman and swerving so much she almost hit the brass statue of the dancer in the roundabout driveway. Madeleine waved back, and then the hairs on the back of her neck stood up. She had a strange feeling of being watched. She flipped around and searched the windows in the building again. Nothing. She shook it off—it had to be nerves.

When she flipped back around to give one last wave to her mom, the old, awful station wagon was gone, leaving only a puff of smoke to remind Madeleine of her old life.

She turned again to the school, her new

home for the next year. Or for as long as she could hold on to the scholarship.

The Dario Quincy Academy of Dance was etched over massive, medieval-looking wooden doors.

She shook her head again to clear away the creepy feeling that was crawling over her. Nerves—nothing more. This was it. She had won a scholarship to the most prestigious ballet school in the country. If the building got up and tried to eat her alive, she would still go in.

Madeleine squared her shoulders and walked up the long, creepy stairs toward her new life.

Chapter 2

"One, two, three, one, two, three, legs up ladies, stomachs in—Kayley, if I see you drop that leg one more time, I swear I will cut it off—and up and two and attitude, onto pointe and . . ."

Madeleine warmed up on the side of the class, stretching her leg on the barre and putting head to knee, all the while watching her new ballet mistress, Madame Puant, work the classroom. Madeleine had met Madame Puant once before, of course, when Madame had seen her audition for the scholarship position. But seeing Madame Puant up close, seeing the talent in the room . . . well, Madeleine's heart dropped. In her old class, she had been far and away the best. The new class would be a very different story. She touched her mother's antique gold necklace, thumbing the silhouette of the grand jeté, and willed herself to calm down.

Four girls did center work as the rest of the class warmed up and stretched. Groups of girls huddled together and whispered—about Madeleine, she could tell. Boys peppered the room here or there. Madeleine had never seen so many guys in a ballet class before. In her hometown, hardly any boys would be caught dead dancing ballet—even though it was one of the most challenging physical activities a body could do, as she'd been happy to tell them. A surge of excitement shot through her. Finally, here she was at a real ballet school.

Madame Puant tapped the piano. "Thank you, Patrick. Per usual, your playing is exquisite. We'll do full company center work now, two groups." She peered from below her eyelids around the room, sizing up every person inside. Madeleine felt herself shrink a little.

Madame pointed to eleven different girls and boys and then to Madeleine. "You are group one. The rest are group two."

One girl in Madeleine's group, beautiful and tall, with a perfect ballet body and long neck, stared at her with narrowed eyes. The girl and three of her friends—Madeleine could already tell these were the belles of the ball—moved to the front of the room. Madeleine took her place behind them.

Madame Puant clapped her hands. "Group one. Let's begin with the following: Start in fifth, prepare out, plié, arabesque en pointe to attitude, fourth, then pique pirouette, pirouette, pirouette, back to fifth, relevé, and down . . ."

Madeleine was amazed at the sheer number of directions Madame listed off just for the center work. She looked around to see if her group seemed to catch it all, and everyone seemed engaged. Some shadowed the words with the moves. Sweat trickled down Madeleine's spine. She did two nervous pliés in first and one relevé just as the pianist began to play. Suddenly, Madeleine felt all eyes on her. She knew as the new girl, she would be scrutinized. This was her first time to dance in front of everyone. She touched her necklace for luck.

But as the first notes tinkled out, as usual, the music took her over and she didn't need luck. Madame's directions came to her like waves on the sea. She hit every move and felt every position, delighting in the way she could propel her body, double-checking the mirror to make sure she was hitting the steps. Her foot in arabesque needed a bigger turnout, but otherwise, she felt good about the exercise. In the mirror, the tall girl glared at her once again, and Madeleine, comfortable in her dance, stared back, keeping her expression friendly.

"Group two now." As Madeleine moved out of the way, she thought she saw Madame Puant give her a little approving smile. She smiled to herself. Maybe this would work after all.

Madeleine tried not to notice the tall girl and her group look at her and whisper. As she leaned down toward the barre, she felt different pairs of eyes on her. She looked out the open classroom door and saw two adults, one woman and one man, standing outside, whispering furiously to each other.

Their eyes were wide and scared. The man's white button-down shirt was untucked, disheveled, his tie askew. The woman wore a long, flowing skirt and kept her hair tied in a bun. She pushed up her glasses and looked away from the practice room. The man continued to stare at Madeleine.

Madeleine stood straight up, and her leg fell off the barre with a clunk. A burst of giggles came from the group of girls across from her. Madeleine blushed and wished she could disappear. When she looked outside the classroom door again, the adults were gone.

"Group one again. Same sequence. Add bourrées to the center, then after the sequence running jeté, jeté, jeté, grand jeté, pirouette out, yes? Space appropriately and go." Madeleine barely had time to get in line before the music started. Once again, the tall gorgeous girl who kept giving her the stink eye stood in front of her. The girl's silky, beautifully bunned head turned, and the gorgeous girl gave Madeleine a wicked smile.

"Don't crowd me, newbie," she whispered. The music started, and the line began to move.

Madeleine shook it off and let the music take her over. She gave the girl in front of her plenty of room, then started her routine. She bourréed to the center and then performed the sequence flawlessly, flipping her arms without thinking to the correct positions, making beautiful curves in the mirror. When the time came for her grand jeté, Madeleine pliéd and then exploded, throwing her legs out in a straight split high in the air, her arms and back curved in a perfect arc. She loved the grand jeté and the feeling it gave her.

And then she landed. Right on the back foot of the girl in front of her.

Madame Puant's voice rang through the music: "Ophelia, switch with Madeleine for the next sequence. Madeleine's jeté is better."

There was a gasp from the rest of the room. For the second time that day, Madeleine wished she could disappear. Madame continued counting for the next group, "One, two, three, tak-tak-tak and a . . ."

The girl, Ophelia, evidently, spun around and hissed, "I told you not to crowd me, you freak."

Ophelia's face was bright red. A knotted strand of hair had come out of her bun. Madeleine had a feeling that Ophelia rarely got corrected.

Ophelia stared at Madeleine's necklace and snorted. "Nice necklace. They don't have style where you come from?"

Now it was Madeleine's turn to go red. And before she could help herself, she said, "They don't have ballet lessons where you come from?"

She had to fight putting her hands over her mouth. She couldn't believe she'd said it.

Ophelia's eyes went wide, and she stepped forward. But before anything could be done, Madame's voice echoed around the room. "OK, now full jumps, two at a time, group one— Madeleine, Ophelia, and go."

As Madeleine took her place, she heard

Ophelia say, "You'll be sorry for that. You better watch yourself, new girl."

Madeleine jumped as far and as high away from her as she could manage.

Chapter 3

Madeleine threw down her shower caddy and flopped on her bed. Her first class at the academy and she'd already made an enemy. And from what she could tell, a bad enemy to have. Couldn't she have pissed off a squirrel or something?

Since Madeleine had arrived midday, she'd managed to miss all the non-dance classes for the day, and she'd only made the second of two ballet classes. Students practiced for six hours a day, from six to nine in the mornings and then from three to six in the afternoons. At six thirty, dinner was served. Even in her room on the second floor of the huge house, Madeleine could smell something delicious cooking in the ballroom. Dinner, she'd been told, was buffet style. Though her stomach growled, the thought of going into the ballroom and facing the girls from practice made her cringe. After class, she had barely made it into the shower before anyone else, and she'd scooted out as fast as possible to avoid any awkward run-ins.

She sat up on the bed just to flop down once again, strands of wet hair landing on her face.

For this night only, maybe she would avoid dinner, sneak in late for something to eat later, and then try to smooth things out at class the next morning. Madeleine threw her arm over her eyes. Not a great start. She played with her necklace and felt a wave of homesickness wash over her.

And then she jumped to her feet. Here she was, at the most prestigious ballet school in the country, and she was feeling sorry for herself.

No way. The least she could do was explore a little while everyone else ate. It wouldn't hurt to get a sense of the gigantic institution she now lived in.

Through her door, Madeleine heard girls walking out of their rooms and voices echoing in the hallway. The school was huge, but all the rooms on Madeleine's floor had been split up into one-person units. When the voices died away, she opened her door, looking tentatively into the hall.

No one stood in the dark hallway. The deep red carpet faded to black as Madeleine glanced down the hall each way. Antique lights that looked like candles flickered at intervals, and Madeleine saw what seemed to be a line of endless doors. Here or there, some girls had tried to decorate their doors, but somehow the hallway resisted any color except deep red—the decorations seemed to get absorbed into the walls. A chill crept down Madeleine's back—the same chill she felt when she first entered the school.

The spiral staircase leading to the dining

room gaped to her left, and she heard the murmur of voices and the occasional spike of a laugh. Clinks of silverware traveled up the stairs. It sounded like life and fun. Madeleine's homesickness came back, full force. For a moment she remembered lunchtime at her old high school, having a table to sit at.

Having friends.

She touched her neck and realized she hadn't put her necklace back on.

Madeleine heard what sounded like a creaky door opening to her right. Lights flickered and the hallway curved so that she couldn't see all the way to the end. She called out, "Hello?"

Silence answered her.

She hesitated in the doorway, then gathered up her courage. Down the staircase, in the dining room, was certain persecution. Down the hall, to the left, was the unknown. Maybe it wouldn't be so bad? Madeleine carefully closed and locked her door.

She tiptoed across the bloodred carpet, keeping her eyes fixed on a darkness that always seemed to curve out of sight. How big was this place anyway? The hallway seemed to go on forever.

She passed a door with a wooden sign that read *OPHELIA*. Her new best friend was only three doors away. Great.

As Madeleine stopped to check out Ophelia's door, decorated with photos of ballet dancers and some band Madeline had never seen before, she heard the creaky door again. She flipped her head to the end of the dark hallway.

"Hello?"

Her voice echoed down the hall.

Madeleine kept walking, slower this time. The roar of dinner was gone. A stillness hung like a thick blanket in its place.

Finally, she reached the end of the hall, the carpet running out and a five-foot stretch of cold marble taking its place. High windows stood above the marble on both sides. At the edge of the marble, Madeleine saw a pair of French doors, curtains draped across them.

Light from the large windows reflected off the shiny floor, throwing shadows everywhere. Madeleine looked back down the hallway, the students' doors disappearing into darkness. She shivered, her hair still wet.

Loud footsteps on the other side of the door made Madeleine jump. She gasped and fell against the wall that held the window. Something from the other side of the curtains cast shadows that looked like feet on the marble.

Running feet.

The footsteps seemed to get louder and faster. Then, just as quickly, they died away. Madeleine grabbed a hold of the door handles and turned, bracing herself for the squeak that she'd heard earlier.

But the knobs wouldn't turn. The door was locked.

She knew the squeak had come from this door. It couldn't have been anything else.

And who was running on the door's other side? More importantly, what were they running from?

Outside, the sun was setting. The courtyard trees' branches seemed twisted and deformed. Through the opposite window, Madeleine could see the statue of the ballet dancer at the front of the school, the one her mom had almost hit. From this angle, the ballerina's body looked twisted, just like the branches of the trees, as if she were writhing in pain. The first dead leaves of fall scraped along the sidewalk, the wind starting to pick up.

Madeleine had that feeling again, the feeling from when she first entered the house. The tingle down the back of her neck. Goosebumps all over her body. She felt chills, even through her thick sweatshirt and Uggs. She began shaking, and she knew this time that it wasn't from her wet hair.

Something was wrong. Something was not right in this house.

She instinctively put her hand to her throat but only touched bare skin. The necklace. She hadn't put it back on.

Something knocked sternly on the doors in front of her.

Madeleine gasped and stumbled backward. Once she regained her footing, she sprinted down the hall back toward her room, all thoughts of exploring gone from her mind.

She ran as fast as she could, her ears primed for any strange sounds, for any running footsteps behind her.

When she reached her room, she fumbled with her key in the lock, then flung open the door, slamming it behind her and locking it again.

She touched her neck again and tried to control her breathing. It was just her imagination. A big house, a bad ballet class, a complete and total life change ... Everything would be just fine. Plus, September always started to get creepy toward the end, with dead leaves and long shadows. She just needed to get her head together. She was probably hungry too. Having not eaten since lunch.

After slowing her breaths, she decided she needed to eat. Some food in her empty stomach would make things normal and erase the last few minutes. She decided to head down to the dining room to see if she could scrounge for some food. A quick look at the clock in her room told her it was only 7:20. Perfect timing— there would probably still be food around but no girls ready to hate her. She could open that door, go out into that hall, and get herself some food. There was nothing there. Nothing at all.

It was just a hallway. Even if her goose bumps were starting up again.

Madeleine realized she should put on her necklace for courage. It would remind her why she was here.

Walking over to her dresser, she started to feel better already. She laughed at herself—how could she have let her mind get away from her? There was nothing wrong with this school. The danger was all in her mind.

She scanned the dresser for her necklace. And then frantically scanned it again.

Nothing. Her necklace was gone.

Chapter 4

"I know it was you."

Madeleine was spitting fire.

She had been up all night, chewing on her hair and waiting to confront Ophelia in the morning. She had sprinted to dance class early so she could talk to Ophelia before the whole class came. At her old school, Madeleine loved getting to class early anyway, just to get her mind in the right place for practice. But today she was on a mission.

Ophelia walked in at 5:42. Evidently, Madeleine wasn't the only ballet dancer who liked to arrive before start time. Madeleine stood up, one pointe shoe half tied and the other half on.

Ophelia jumped when she heard Madeleine. Then she put her hands on her hips and said, in a snotty voice. "What?"

Madeleine didn't think she'd ever heard so much venom injected in a word. She swallowed. This was important. This was her family's necklace.

"I know you stole it. And I want it back. Now."

For a moment, Madeleine thought she saw real confusion in Ophelia's face. It turned to disgust.

"Why would I ever steal anything of yours, freak?"

Ophelia threw down her bag in another corner, then took out her pointe shoes and warmers and started dressing like she didn't have a care in the world. She bent over one leg in a long stretch. Madeleine knew she'd been dismissed. The fire in her belly grew.

She stomped over to Ophelia. "That necklace has been in my family for years! You saw it yesterday, and you're mad that I'm a better dancer than you. So you stole my necklace when I left my room. And I want it back. Now!"

Ophelia sat up slowly. "A better dancer than me?"

Madeleine could see the veins in Ophelia's neck. "Just because you can jump high doesn't make you a better dancer. You better watch yourself around here. You're not in some podunk town anymore, *scholarship* girl. There are *real* dancers here."

Madeleine became vaguely aware of other dancers trickling in, felt their stares. *Scholarship*—she had thought that was a secret. She lifted up her chin.

"Yeah, well, there are real jerks here too, evidently. And real thieves."

Ophelia's friends drifted over to her corner. Out of the corner of Madeleine's eye, Madame Puant came in, followed by Patrick, the pianist. Madeleine glanced back at her bag. She needed to get ready.

"All I know," she said, "is I'd better get that necklace back. And you better do it soon."

Ophelia narrowed her eyes. "I'm. So. Scared."

Madeleine glared at Ophelia one last time, and some of the girls around her giggled. She didn't care. She'd never been so mad in all her life. When Madame started them on barre exercises, Madeleine threw herself into the warm-ups, trying to use the fire for her dancing. After classes ended, she would find a way to get Ophelia back.

***

"Madeleine, there's an empty seat by the wall. There you go."

Madeleine made her way to the back of the class, feeling all eyes on her. She had already been introduced to everyone, of course. They'd all been at ballet practice too. But even so, Madeleine still felt the shame of the first-day student.

Mr. Barnes, the English teacher, gave her a kind smile. He was the same man who had stared at her at practice the other day. He still looked untidy and a little like he never slept, but Madeleine was just grateful that *someone* was showing her some kindness. He winked a fatherly wink and then suddenly put his hand up to his nose. "Just a minute, everybody. You'll have to excuse me."

He left the class to murmurs and quizzical looks. *Oh great*, thought Madeleine. *The first person to be nice to me sprints out of the room.*

The girl in front of Madeleine turned around and said, "Mr. Barnes is new. He leaves class, like, three times an hour. It's weird. But he's still super cool. I think he's my favorite."

Madeleine was so startled that someone her age was talking to her that all she said was, "Oh."

The girl smiled. "I'm Kayley."

Madeleine recognized Kayley as one of the girls that hung around Ophelia. Was this a trick?

As if Kayley had read Madeleine's face, she said, "Yeah, I'm friends with Ophelia. But she's not that bad, really. She was just jealous of you. Don't let her get to you. You're a *really* good dancer, and she's used to being the best. It's good for her to have to work harder." She grinned at Madeleine.

Madeleine couldn't help but smile back. She always liked to hear she was a good dancer, but more importantly, this person didn't hate her! She snuck a peek at Ophelia and saw she was looking over at them. That made her smile too.

She turned back to Kayley, who had taken out a pack of Twizzlers and started gnawing on one.

"I think Ophelia stole my necklace," Madeleine blurted out. She swallowed, embarrassed she'd said that to one of Ophelia's friends.

Kayley's face scrunched and she just shook her head. "No, that doesn't sound like her. If she doesn't like you, she goes cold, not hot. She'd just freeze you out and pretend you didn't exist."

It did seem like Ophelia was cold, Madeleine thought. And for whatever reason, she felt she could trust Kayley.

Before Madeleine could reply, Mr. Barnes walked in again. Even from the back of the class, Madeleine could see a red smudge under his nose. He looked terrible, possibly worse than before.

With a hoarse voice but a big smile he said, "OK, my favorite class! *Catcher in the Rye*. Who read it? Any phonies in here? If you're faking, I'll spot it."

Madeleine smiled at him. She'd read the book so she caught onto the joke. And Mr. Barnes actually sounded like he would teach a fun class. Maybe class here wouldn't be so bad after all.

***

After class—a fun one, like Madeleine thought— he called her name as everyone else left.

He looked at her with soft, compassionate eyes. "Madeleine, how has your first day been?"

Without warning, a lump formed in her throat. "It's been OK," she said. She put her hand up to her collar, but the lack of a necklace almost made her lose it completely.

Mr. Barnes shifted his briefcase and tapped his hand on his leg. He looked at Madeleine with such kindness that a tear actually escaped her eye.

"First days are always hard," he said. "It will get better here. I promise. We are all here to keep you safe. You can always talk to any of the teachers. Anytime."

Madeleine nodded.

"I mean it," Mr. Barnes said. He smiled again. Madeleine couldn't help but smile back. Then he turned on his heel and left.

Even though the day had started off pretty badly, at least she had a good teacher to count on. And a possible—she wouldn't let herself think *probable*—friend in Kayley.

As Madeleine walked to her room, she thought about what Kayley had said about Ophelia. Her gut told her to trust the girl. But if Ophelia hadn't stolen her necklace, then who had?

Chapter 5

Madeleine was exhausted after the second ballet class of the day. She'd had to do eight—eight!—fouettés in a row, and she and Ophelia had been the only ones able to complete them all. She was also exhausted from all the hard stares she and Ophelia had been exchanging. Her legs were sore and so was her heart. Still no sign of her necklace.

Soon, smells from the kitchen wafted under Madeleine's door, and she sat up. No way was she going to miss dinner tonight. She was way too hungry. She put on her fluffy boots and went downstairs. At two minutes until the official mealtime, no one else sat in the dining room. Madeleine went to the buffet area, loaded up her plate, and then chickened out. Taking the stairs two at a time back to her room, she managed to avoid anyone coming out for dinner.

Tomorrow. Tomorrow she'd go to dinner with everyone else.

After she finished eating, she got out her phone and looked at the photos she had taken over the last couple of years, a lot of them from her house and with her mom. As an only child from a single mother, she was crazy close to her mom. She reached again for her necklace and only felt her empty chest where the necklace was supposed to sit. She started to cry.

She didn't realize chasing her dream would be so lonely.

Then, in an instant, she was asleep. The drain of the day and the deep homesickness she felt had taken their toll, and her eyes just wouldn't stay open. When she jolted awake, the room was completely dark. The illuminated lights on the alarm clock said eleven thirty.

She lunged upright when she heard a loud bump just outside her window. Her second-floor window?

The bump came again, and her window rattled.

Her heart pounding, Madeleine moved slowly toward the window. With a shaking hand, she reached out to pull open one of the drapes as a loud *thunk* sounded. Madeleine screeched and jumped back.

The *thunk* turned into a pounding, and she heard a voice say, "Let me in, let me in. Hurry."

This was definitely not something supernatural. This was one of her fellow students.

Scenarios rushed through her mind: a serial killer on the loose and stalking ballet students; a rabid dog mauling someone on the grounds; the statue of the ballet dancer, twisted and shadowy, coming to life and menacing a classmate . . .

She threw open the window and saw a long leg climb over the ledge, then another, until the figure had entered her room. And then she stood face-to-face with Ophelia.

Madeleine narrowed her eyes. "You."

Ophelia glanced back through the window and waved her hand for something outside to get going.

"So this is how you got in to steal my necklace?" Madeleine said.

Ophelia blew out a gust of air and checked over her shoulder again. "Oh for the love of god, I didn't steal your necklace. Why would I care?"

Before Madeleine could respond, a knock sounded on the door. Madeleine's heart sped up again. Who would be knocking at this hour? Ophelia hurriedly closed the window and drapes and then flipped around, giving Madeleine a look she didn't quite understand.

The knock came again. Madeleine rushed to the door and opened it.

Madame Puant stood in the hallway in a robe and slippers. Madeleine was startled. Not just because Madame had shown up at her door at eleven thirty but because Madame was wearing something else other than leggings and gauzy scarves.

Madame looked past Madeleine to Ophelia, who sat on the bed with an innocent expression on her face, one of Madeleine's textbooks open in front of her. She chirped, "Hi, Madame."

Madame narrowed her eyes. "Curfew is at ten. No exceptions, even for homework. *If* that's what you're doing."

Madame turned the full force of her stare to Madeleine. "It seems someone saw one of our students getting out of a car and running into the building. I don't suppose either of you would know anything about that."

Madeleine turned to Ophelia. Ophelia's eyes were just a bit too bright. She said, way too cheerily, "No, Madame. We haven't seen anything."

Madame turned to Madeleine, squinting at her as if trying to get into her very soul. "And you, Madeleine? Have you seen anyone? Remember that to lie to an administrator at this school is to be expelled."

Anger flared up inside Madeleine. Not only

had Ophelia stolen her necklace and made her first three days miserable, she also just put Madeleine in a position to be expelled. She couldn't lose her scholarship. She just couldn't. Now would be the time to get Ophelia back.

She straightened her back and prepared to tell Madame the truth. And then her heart sank.

Madeleine was just not that person. She wouldn't rat Ophelia out, no matter how awful the girl had been.

She cleared her throat and looked at the floor. "No. I haven't seen anything, Madame."

When she looked back up, Madame's stare drilled a hole in her. But Madeleine saw something else too. Something that looked suspiciously like respect.

"Very well, then," Madame said. "I'm sure you girls would let me know if something was amiss. At Dario, we take integrity very seriously. Curfew must be followed. And we are a team of dancers—no matter what competition entails. We must work as a group and depend on one another. I'm glad to see you girls finding that sense of teamwork. Even after curfew. Ophelia,

I expect you in bed no more than five minutes from now. If I catch you out of curfew again, there will be severe consequences."

"Yes, Madame," Ophelia said quietly.

And then Madame shut the door. Madeleine stared at the black, old-fashioned doorknob and lock. She took a deep breath, barely registering her blank white walls and her secondhand suitcases with duct tape still on the scuffed wooden floor. Her dressing table and mirror had only one picture: she'd put one up of her and her mom.

She sat still for a minute, trying not to scream at Ophelia.

When she turned around, Ophelia was standing up, the haughty look she normally wore completely gone.

"Why did you do that?"

Madeleine gave up any more thoughts of a fight. She was too tired to worry about anything anymore. She sat down at her dressing table chair and shrugged.

"I don't tell on people. Even if they do suck."

To Madeleine's surprise, Ophelia laughed.

"OK, I'll admit I've been pretty sucky to you since you got here."

Her blue eyes wide and sincere, she continued: "But you have to believe that I didn't steal your necklace. In fact, that's why I was out tonight. Someone stole a ring of mine. I'm pretty sure. I thought maybe I'd left it at a friend's house the last time I snuck out. But it's not there either. And I believe my friend."

"Maybe you just lost it," Madeleine said, shrugging.

Ophelia's haughty look returned instantly. "Maybe you just lost your necklace?"

"OK, good point. But was your ring a family heirloom? Or worth a lot of money? My necklace wasn't, but it is . . . important to me."

Ophelia nodded. "Mine isn't an heirloom, but it's special to me, like your necklace is to you. My grandma gave it to me. It's cheap and costumey, so I don't know why anyone would steal it. But it's gone. And just like your necklace, I *know* I didn't lose it. I would never."

Madeleine nodded. She believed Ophelia. For the first time since Madeleine had met her,

Ophelia looked downright vulnerable.

She slumped down. "Is there a thief at Dario, do you think?"

"I think there is," Ophelia said. "This school . . . well, it's got a personality of its own, that's for sure. Things are not right here."

Madeleine was about to agree when a knock sounded at the door.

Madame's voice thundered through the wood. "Back to bed, Ophelia."

Both girls jumped, and Ophelia grinned. "Better get going." She opened the door, then looked both ways down the empty hallway. Madeleine wondered how Madame Puant could move so fast.

Ophelia turned back to Madeleine. "We need to find our stuff and who is taking it," she whispered. "Tomorrow night we are exploring this place."

Madeleine raised an eyebrow. "Like in people's rooms?"

Ophelia shook her head. "I don't think it's our classmates stealing these things."

"Then who?"

Ophelia's eyes flickered along with the hall's antique lights. "I think it's the house itself. I think we're dealing with a ghost."

With that, she disappeared down the red carpet, leaving Madeleine to shiver alone in her room.

Chapter 6

Madeleine didn't believe in ghosts. At least that's what she told herself all night alone in her room.

It didn't work. She barely slept a wink. She kept remembering the hallway's strange shadows and the footsteps she had heard on the other side of the curtained French doors. She remembered looking out the window and seeing the bronze dancer twisting grotesquely in the shadows.

For a while, she wondered if Ophelia was just

messing with her. But she had always trusted her instincts, and they told her that Ophelia owed her one and knew it. And she had a feeling that not only did Ophelia not want to owe her but also that she might even want to be her friend.

The thought brought a smile to Madeleine. Maybe the academy wouldn't be so horrible after all. She had two maybe-friends, at least one great teacher, and a helluva grand jeté. This could be a great school.

Even with a ghost.

* * *

The next morning, Madeleine walked shyly into the studio, ten minutes later than she normally did, her eyes a dark baggy mess. A quick look at Ophelia and Madeleine knew she hadn't slept well either. When their eyes met, Ophelia said, "Madeleine, put your stuff here."

Madeleine had to hold in her surprised grin.

"Madeleine, this is Emma and Sophie," Ophelia said, waving to two other girls in her corner. "They're twins, fraternal." Madeleine couldn't believe how different they looked.

Emma had red hair and freckles. Sophie had super dark hair and eyebrows, dramatic against her pale skin. The only thing the two girls had in common were their startling blue eyes.

"Hi, Madeleine," they said perkily, in unison. Madeleine tried not to be freaked out.

"And this is Kayley," Ophelia said. Kayley winked at Madeleine, her brown eyes twinkling.

"Oh, Madeleine and I had a heart-to-heart in English." She grinned at Ophelia, who did her best to remain haughty looking. "I was telling her that you suck in a lot of ways, but you're no thief."

Kayley took out a Twizzler and started eating it. Ophelia snatched it away.

"This is going to make you sugar crash, and you know Madame is going to make us fouetté a billion times today." She threw the half-eaten Twizzler in the garbage, ignoring Kayley's indignant, "Hey!"

Ophelia turned to Madeleine. "Kayley may be a little blunt and misguided, but she's right. I didn't steal anything. Which brings me to my next point."

Madeleine leaned in. The other three girls did too.

"Madeleine, when was your necklace stolen?" Ophelia continued.

"The first night I was here."

"Yes, but *when*?"

Madeleine paused for a second. "It happened during dinner. I didn't go down to eat, but I sort of half-explored the hallway."

Ophelia shot a knowing look at the other girls, who all nodded. "We all had something stolen at the same time. Ours was during dinner, when we were in the dining room. So I think later on tonight, we go exploring."

Madeleine crinkled her eyebrows. "Where? We have no idea who might be doing this and no idea where to look."

Ophelia leaned in. "Well, I don't think it's the girls here, because there's no way anyone can hide anything for long in this place. And the boys can't even access this wing."

"Seriously," Kayley said. "Everyone is in everyone's business. You can't sneeze without somebody knowing."

"So we can rule out the second floor," Ophelia said. She flipped her hair. "And none of our things were super expensive or anything. They just meant something to each of us."

It was true, Madeleine thought. Her necklace wouldn't be worth anything to anyone else. It was just something personal for her. She wondered what had been stolen from everyone else.

She asked Kayley, "What was stolen from you?"

"A pair of gloves I got from my grandma. They're all torn and stained, so no one would want them. Except me, because my grandma passed away two years ago." For once Kayley's mischievous grin disappeared. Emma rubbed her shoulder.

Madeleine looked at Emma and Sophie. "And you two?"

"Our grandpa's pocket watch," said Emma.

"Our grandma's locket, with a picture of her and our grandpa together. It plays 'Let Me Call You Sweetheart,'" said Sophie.

Kayley rubbed the twins' shoulders in turn.

"Yeah, that's weird," Madeleine said. "They're all old or something too. Has anyone else had anything stolen?"

Ophelia waved her hand. "Oh, who cares about anyone else? The main thing is *we* have." As Ophelia leaned in, Madame Puant entered the room and tapped her cane on the ground.

"Barre work, everyone! You were sloppy yesterday, and I want to see perfect turn out, perfect pointed toes, and deep pliés. No cheating. That means you, Kayley."

Kayley rolled her eyes and looked to her bag. Probably for another Twizzler, Madeleine thought.

Then Madeleine realized she hadn't even put on her shoes. She sat down fast and began suiting up.

While the piano player came in and started warming up with some scales, Emma, Sophie, Kayley, Ophelia, and Madeleine rushed to tie up their pointe shoes.

"Madeleine's right," Ophelia whispered. "Everything stolen was old and family-related but nothing expensive. So who would want to steal these things?"

All four of them shrugged.

Ophelia's eyes sparkled. "A ghost, that's who! So tonight we go ghost hunting."

When Madame slammed her cane into the ground again, all five of them jumped.

Chapter 7

In English, Madeleine whispered to Kayley, "Where are we going to be hunting this 'ghost'?"

Kayley shrugged. "Ophelia loves to be dramatic."

As if she could hear them from the other side of the room, Ophelia squinted at them. Kayley pulled out a Tootsie Pop and gnawed on it.

"Do you think there are ghosts here?"

"Something is weird here. I don't know what it is, but this place isn't right. I don't know if it's a ghost, but I know something feels strange."

Madeleine nodded. "I felt that way my very first night."

At that moment, Mr. Barnes appeared in the doorway with Ms. Jamison, both of them staring at each other intently.

Kayley pointed at them with the Tootsie Pop. "We can't even keep teachers here. Both of those guys are new, and so is our physics teacher."

Mr. Barnes and Ms. Jamison seemed to be arguing with each other, Ms. Jamison throwing her hands up and Mr. Barnes shaking his head. Madeleine kept one eye on them, feeling a little protective of Mr. Barnes, and said, "Do you think Mr. Barnes is OK? He seems so nice, but he looks, like strung out."

Mr. Barnes walked in the room as Madeleine finished her sentence.

Before Kayley turned back around, she said, "Yeah, he's my favorite teacher here. But he definitely seems strung out. We'll have to solve *that* mystery after we catch the ghost! . . . So Ophelia told you where to meet tonight, right?"

Madeleine shook her head.

"Duh. She probably doesn't have your number yet. She texted us. Which is kind of dumb because texts don't go through the walls of this place most of the time. The reception is all wonky. Anyway, we're meeting at the end of the hall on the second floor. By those French doors."

Madeleine shivered. She remembered the doors and echoes of running footsteps behind them.

"What time?"

"What other time?" Kayley grinned. "Midnight, of course."

Just then, Mr. Barnes said, "All right, class. Let's jump into some Poe. As you know, he was obsessed with death, and most of his poetry reflects this. But who doesn't like a little bit of death on a fall afternoon?"

The class laughed a little, and Mr. Barnes's eyes twinkled. Even so, Madeleine still thought he looked like death warmed over. His eyes were red rimmed, and his nose had that same raw look underneath as before. He looked tired.

They would definitely have to figure out what was going on with him next. Madeleine knew good teachers were hard to come by.

Nothing in this place was normal, Madeleine thought. Then she chuckled to herself. Instead of running away, she was going hunting for danger. At midnight.

***

When the clock struck 11:56, Madeleine's nerves hit an all-time high. At dinner, she'd sat with Kayley, Emma, Sophie, and Ophelia, and they'd formulated a barebones plan.

Meet at midnight at the end of the hall.

Make sure no hall monitors were out.

Bring a flashlight.

Wear a sweatshirt.

Bring a phone in case of emergency.

Bring chalk.

Madeleine double-checked her bag. She had everything.

When she'd asked Ophelia during dinner why they needed chalk, Ophelia said, "In case we need to write arrows to figure out the way back."

Kayley, in what Madeleine was beginning to consider her signature move, rolled her eyes again. "God, Ophelia, it's just the basement. We're not exploring caves or anything."

"It's the *deep* basement, Kayley, not the props basement," Ophelia had replied. "I'm talking boiler room. I've seen the stairs on the far side of the props room."

Sophie chimed in, "Why are we going to the boiler-room basement?"

Then it had been Ophelia's turn to roll her eyes. "Because, where else would a ghost hide?"

Emma shook her head. "I'm not so sure . . ."

"Look, it's not going to hurt to check it out, right?" Ophelia pleaded. "And anyway, it will give us some adventure. We can figure out a hiding place down there or something if we need it." Her eyes flashed. "Plus, how secret agent will this be?"

Kayley snorted. "Yeah. Fun."

Ophelia glared at her. "Then don't come."

Kayley shrugged. Madeleine had been able to tell there was no way she'd miss this adventure.

"I should come just so you losers don't get into trouble."

Madeleine had to hide a smile. She could almost feel Ophelia's need for some sort of action. And why would it hurt to go exploring? Besides the expulsion that would obviously take place if they got caught . . .

Madeleine shook off that thought. Anyway, if their stolen things weren't in the basement, maybe they'd be in the prop room. Besides, she really wanted to see what all the school held. And she had friends now. No way was she giving that up.

"So, midnight then?" she said to Ophelia.

"Midnight. Bring the stuff we talked about. And no telling *anyone* about this. It's just for us."

As the clock moved to 11:57, Madeleine wondered if she'd made the right decision.

She took a deep breath and patted her bag. "Well, it's too late to duck out now," she said. "Time to hunt a ghost."

And then she stepped out the door into the dark, endless hallway, toward the door of her nightmares.

Chapter 8

A tap on Madeleine's shoulder made her shriek. A hand wrapped itself around her mouth, and before she kicked the person, she recognized Kayley's whisper: "Jeez, calm down! You're making a ton of noise."

Kayley relaxed her hand and let go. Madeleine stepped back and tried to control her breathing.

"You scared the crap out of me!" she whispered furiously.

"Clearly." Kayley chewed on a gummy worm.

Out of spite, Madeleine grabbed the candy and threw it down.

"Hey!" Kayley said, but before she could retaliate, Ophelia, Sophie, and Emma materialized out of the shadows.

Ophelia scanned the abandoned hall. Then, satisfied, she whispered, "Did everyone bring their stuff?"

Everyone nodded. Madeleine could see the excitement and dread in everyone's faces. It was exactly how she felt.

Ophelia said, "Let's go."

Adrenaline spiked through Madeleine's body. Ophelia produced an old-fashioned key from a pocket and unlocked the French doors.

Madeleine said, "Where did you—"

Before she could finish, Ophelia waved the question away.

"Not important. What is is that I have it." She walked through the French doors and Madeleine followed. Madeleine felt Kayley grab the back of her shirt, and Madeleine grabbed Ophelia's in turn.

"I don't want to be in back," Emma whispered.

"Don't be such a baby!" Sophie said.

But Madeleine didn't blame her. The hallway behind the door was, if possible, even creepier than the stretch outside her room. The only lighting came from high windows that let strange shadows spill onto the floor. High windows and a single bright red Exit sign that shone at the hallway's end. If Madeleine was going to turn back, now was the time. It was either suck it up and hunt a ghost or turn back. She swallowed and held on more tightly to Ophelia's sweatshirt.

Ophelia stopped for a second and turned to the others. "I'm pretty sure that Exit sign marks the stairs to the basement."

"Pretty sure?" Kayley whispered.

"Well, I've only been down here once!" Ophelia snapped. "And I never went through the door. We're just going to have to try it."

Kayley huffed, but Madeleine said, "We've already opened the door. We might as well see where it leads."

Ophelia smiled at her, then turned around, and the five of them turned into a chain again.

When they reached the exit, Ophelia touched her hand to the door.

"Wait!" Emma said.

"Now what?" Ophelia said impatiently.

"What if an alarm goes off?"

"Well, be ready to run," Kayley replied, and Ophelia squared her shoulders and pushed through the door.

Nothing happened.

Madeleine let go of a breath she'd been holding and resumed her place behind Ophelia. The group climbed down the dangerously dark concrete stairs until there were none left, and Ophelia pulled up the door's latch.

The room was completely dark.

The air felt close and musty, like the inside of a coffin. Madeleine held tight onto Ophelia's shirt.

She heard rustling behind her and then saw a flashlight beam go on. Then two more. She rummaged through her own bag and flicked on her own light. The beams began to scan the room.

The place, full of dark silhouettes, came to life. They were in the prop room.

Madeleine saw peasant outfits on one rack—she recognized them as costumes for *Giselle*. Her eyes moved to glittery masks and sleighs and a giant present she knew must be for *The Nutcracker*...This was a perfect room.

She heard a squeal and spun around. Her flashlight landed on Emma, who had thrown on a sparkly tiara and a boa.

"I'm Sleeping Beauty!" she cried. Everyone laughed. And as if a starting gun had gone off, they all scattered to look at different costumes.

"Look for antiquey things!" Madeleine said. "This might be the perfect place to hide our stuff."

Ophelia put the flashlight under her chin and cackled. "Or to find a ghost!"

Madeleine roamed around, drawn to the costumes at the back of the room, the ones she knew came from *Giselle*. When she was close enough to inspect the costumes, though, she saw they were yellowed with age and covered in dust. Every prestigious school danced *Giselle*.

Maybe she had just missed the newer costumes.

"Don't touch those." Madeleine almost jumped out of her skin.

Ophelia stood next to her. Out of the darkness, her voice shook. "These costumes haven't been used since . . ."

Before Ophelia could finish the sentence, Kayley's voice rang out.

"You guys. I think I found the door to the boiler room."

It was old and wooden and crossed with metal bars, like some medieval torture chamber door. Ophelia reached out her hand to turn the knob, and the door swung open. Their five flashlights illuminated a narrow hallway and a set of old, stone steps, each and every step cracked and crumbling. The smell of mold, mildew, and graves crept into Madeleine's nose.

After a moment of silence, Ophelia looked to the rest of them. "Well, it's time to find our ghost."

Chapter 9

More than ever, Madeleine wondered if the ghost hunt was such a great idea. She turned to Kayley, who turned to Sophie, who turned to Emma. Ophelia stared down the stairs, gathering her courage.

She started downward without a word.

Madeleine grabbed at the tail of Ophelia's sweatshirt, flashlight in her other hand. She felt Kayley grab her sweatshirt as the other girls assumed the formation. The staircase was so narrow they could only go single file anyway. No one spoke.

Ophelia reached the bottom of the stairs, where another medieval-looking door stood before her. She turned the knob and swung the door open. Madeleine held on tight, then gasped.

Lights flickered above them. Ophelia turned around with her mouth agape and looked at her. Madeleine knew they were thinking the same thing: was someone else down there?

Ophelia turned back around and moved on, and in a moment, the girls found themselves in a stone tunnel, walls dark with what looked like soot or charcoal. Candles flickered at even intervals down the path, real ones, not electric lights like on the second floor. Up ahead, the tunnel appeared to break off in different directions.

Kayley whispered, "What in the world?"

Emma looked with big eyes at the other girls. "Maybe not this world."

Ophelia gave her a withering stare. "Emma. Ghosts wouldn't light candles. Or need them."

"What if it's a teacher?" Sophie said. "Or Madame Puant?"

Ophelia shook her head. "Look, what teacher is here at midnight? I'm guessing it's some janitor or cook or someone who hides out down here."

"But what about the whole heirloom thing?" Madeleine said. "And the ghost?"

Ophelia shrugged. "Well, I'm not writing off the ghost just yet. But if it's some janitor, who knows? Maybe they have an antique fetish or something? Whatever. Let's go figure it out."

She started down the hall, but no one followed.

"Well?"

Madeleine spoke up: "Ophelia . . ."

"What." Ophelia's haughty expression was back.

"Someone is down here. Someone that could possibly get us in trouble." Out of the corner of her eye, Madeleine saw Kayley nodding.

"I was all for this when I thought it might be a ghost, but now, if they see us, well . . . I can't lose my scholarship."

Ophelia's shoulders slumped, and Madeleine took a big breath. She had taken a huge chance speaking out. But when she looked at everyone around her, all she saw were sympathetic looks. Even from Ophelia.

"All right," Ophelia said. "Let's go back. It's not worth it. Besides," she said, her haughty look returning, "the reason these candles are here is probably actually really boring."

Madeleine felt her whole body relax and watched Emma, Sophie, and Kayley ease up at the same time.

And then they heard the scream.

Chapter 10

Every muscle in Madeleine's body told her to run, yet she felt somehow paralyzed.

A look at all the girls told her they felt the same.

Sophie was the first one to speak. "What was that?"

"We have to help whoever it was," Kayley said.

"Nuh-uh. No way," Emma said. "That wasn't a scream you want to be a part of."

Ophelia stomped toward Emma. "Don't be a baby! We need to help whoever that was."

Madeleine's adrenaline rush was slowly dissipating. "They're right, Emma. We need to find who that was and make sure they're OK."

Sophie rubbed Emma's shoulder. "We're all scared, Em."

Emma gulped. "You're right." New strength came into her voice. "Where did the scream come from?"

"I think it came from the left, from that tunnel over there. Come on!" Ophelia said.

All five girls jogged down the hall. When they got to the entrance of the left passageway, they saw that it split off into still more tunnels.

Ophelia whispered, "Sophie, Emma, Kayley, you take that branch. Madeleine and I will take this one. Keep your phones on and your flashlights ready."

"Why do we need our flashlights?" Kayley said. "There are candles everywhere."

"To knock someone in the head if you need to. OK, let's go."

Madeleine and Ophelia crept along the

stone floor quietly and slowly. The smell of mold was so powerful that Madeleine's nose almost couldn't take it. She felt she would sneeze at any moment. She rubbed her nose. Why was this happening now of all times? Her eyes watered, and she brushed at them impatiently.

Suddenly, Madeleine almost ran into Ophelia as Ophelia stopped in her tracks. "Did you hear that?" she whispered.

Madeleine shook her head. Then she did hear it. The sound of many people chanting.

Ophelia looked at her with wide eyes, put a finger to her lips, and started down the hall again. Madeleine followed, wondering for the billionth time if this was a good idea and still suppressing a sneeze.

The chanting got louder and more eerie, keening and wailing, one voice louder than the rest speaking in a language Madeleine didn't understand. Finally, she and Ophelia came to an archway toward a room where the chanting seemed to be coming from. Ophelia crouched down on one side of the arch, and Madeleine followed her.

An altar of some sort stood in the center of the room with a strange symbol carved into it. Six hooded figures surrounded the table, holding dripping candles and chanting. Torches lit the room from wooden mounts on the wall. Through a gap in the formation of the hooded figures, Madeleine could barely make out the items on top of the altar—which included her necklace.

The same scream the girls had heard earlier pierced the chanting.

A female figure writhed on the ground near the altar. A deep male voice rang out, this time in English.

"She feels it again! Rejoice, for our plans will be realized! Rejoice!"

Madeleine felt Ophelia shudder, and her own terror had reached a fever pitch. *Our plans will be realized?* Nothing good could come of that. Her nose started itching, and she rubbed it furiously.

But this time, there was nothing she could do. With horror, she felt her body contract.

She sneezed.

After that, everything happened so fast, she wasn't sure what was real and what wasn't.

The chanting stopped. Madeleine and Ophelia began to run.

Madeleine had never run so fast in her life, and she still could barely keep up with Ophelia.

In the main hallway, they ran headfirst into Kayley, Emma, and Sophie.

"What's going on? Why are you running?" Emma cried.

With terror in her eyes, Ophelia pointed to the hooded figures running toward them. All five girls took off down the hall again.

Sprinting as fast as they could, they made it back to the boiler room door, climbed the narrow cement stairs, and tore through the prop room. When they reached the hallway on the second floor, they sprinted to the French doors and opened them in a panic. With trembling hands, Ophelia got out the key and locked it again.

"What . . . the . . . ," Kayley managed to get out.

The sound of footsteps echoed on the other side of the door. The girls sprinted down the hallway and ran into the closest room—Sophie's.

Ophelia kept her ear to the door to hear if anyone was coming. After fifteen minutes with no noises, Sophie turned on the light and all five girls collapsed.

"Well," Kayley said. "We can safely say we don't have a ghost."

"Yeah," Ophelia said, "no ghost. Just a murderous cult."

Chapter 11

At ballet class the next morning, Madeleine felt like she'd been run over by a truck.

After decompressing for a couple hours, everyone had gone back to their rooms to try to get some sleep.

Madeleine didn't get a wink. Hooded figures kept running at her whenever she closed her eyes, and "Rejoice!" echoed through her mind.

Now, tying their pointe shoes, Kayley and Ophelia were having the same argument they'd had the night before.

Kayley whispered furiously, "Ophelia. Listen to reason. We saw a freaking cult last night! We need to tell Madame Puant."

"And get expelled? No thank you."

Sophie chimed in, "But Ophelia, this is big. They are stealing our stuff and using it for . . ." She shivered.

"For who knows what!" Emma said.

Madeleine stood with Ophelia. She knew she couldn't lose her scholarship. "What did we really see? Maybe it's their religion or something, and we interrupted their worship . . . uh, ceremony."

Kayley rolled her eyes. "Yeah, a worship ceremony. With our stolen stuff. You guys, how did these people get into our school? And what are they doing?"

Sophie nodded. "I'm scared."

At that moment, Madame Puant walked in and banged her cane on the floor. "Barre exercises, everyone. Trey, I saw you slacking off yesterday. Not again."

"We'll talk more at lunch," Ophelia said

under her breath. "I'm scared too," she added.

She squeezed Kayley's hand, who squeezed Sophie's, who squeezed Emma's. Emma reached out to Madeleine, and Madeleine felt a warm glow spread through her.

"We're in this together," whispered Ophelia. And Madeleine, despite the crazy night, despite the fact that a murderous cult may be out to kill her, felt better than she had since arriving at the academy's doors.

She had friends.

Just then Trey burst through them in a pirouette to the barre.

"Get a room," he said. Every one of them cracked up as he spun past the group.

***

In English, Madeleine's body ached. Her head felt like it would explode. One look at Kayley and the rest of the girls told her they felt the same way.

Mr. Barnes rushed in looking like Madeleine felt. She wondered if he, too, had had a long night.

"Onto more Poe, class! Your papers were pretty po', so we'll have to look over his work again."

The class groaned. But Madeleine saw that the usual twinkle in the teacher's eye was gone.

Kayley turned around and grinned at Madeleine. Madeleine gasped: "Kayley, your nose."

"What?" Kayley asked and wiped under it. Bright red blood colored her hand.

"Holy—." She looked at Madeleine. "Madeleine, you . . ."

But Madeleine had already felt the first drips of blood. Across the room, Ophelia held her nose too. And Sophie and Emma.

Mr. Barnes stopped his lecture and pulled out a huge stash of Kleenex from his desk drawer. He handed the tissues to each of them.

"OK, girls, to the infirmary," he said.

Madeleine hoped he didn't wonder why all five of them had bloody noses at the same time. How could this have happened?

The girls began their walk down the hall to the infirmary, staring at one another in confusion above big balls of Kleenex.

"What is going on?" Sophie asked.

"*Now* should we tell someone?" Kayley said to Ophelia through her wadded-up Kleenex.

"Tell them what?" Ophelia said.

Kayley sighed in exasperation. "About last night! Do you think it's a coincidence that we *all* have nosebleeds?"

"So we say the cult attacked our sinuses? Grow up, Kayley!"

Before Kayley could respond, they reached the infirmary and the nurse came out. This was the first time Madeleine had met him, but all the other girls said, "Hey, Nurse John."

"Well, this looks like trouble with a capital *T*." He smiled and dimples appeared. Madeleine thought he was the best-looking nurse she had ever seen. Maybe the best-looking *guy* she had ever seen. She would try to be sick more often, she decided. She caught Kayley smiling at her madly behind a Kleenex and kicked her lightly.

"Well, come in and we'll take a look," Nurse John said. "All five of you have nosebleeds?"

They nodded their heads. "Well, that's

unusual. Come in. Lie back, but not all the way back. Keep pinching your nose—the bleeding'll end soon."

Madeleine lay against a pillow on one of the infirmary beds and thought about the events of the past couple days. She couldn't deny that it was strange they all had nosebleeds at the same time. And she couldn't deny that it didn't bode well for the days ahead.

Chapter 12

By the time everyone's nosebleed had stopped, it was lunchtime. The girls reconvened outside the infirmary.

"I want to put my bag away. Let's all meet by the stairs, then go to lunch," Ophelia said.

"We're not done with this conversation," Kayley grumbled. "I still think we should tell someone."

Borrowing Kayley's move, Ophelia rolled her eyes. "We'll talk more about it at lunch."

When Madeleine got back to her room, she crawled into bed without even taking off her shoes. She was so tired. All she wanted to do was sleep.

But the shriek from Ophelia's room brought her out of her sleepy reverie.

She ran to Ophelia's room and barged in without knocking. Ophelia's face was stark white as she stared at her dressing table. On top of it sat five dolls that looked a little like each of the girls. Each of them had pins stuck right in their hearts. Bloodred smears surrounded the pins.

Madeleine put her hand to her mouth. Just then, Kayley, Emma, and Sophie came to the room and knocked into her. She heard each of them gasp, in turn.

Emma whispered, "Is that blood?"

"I don't want to find out," Sophie said.

Kayley looked at Ophelia. "*Now* do we tell someone?"

Ophelia, face still pale, turned slowly toward her. "Yeah, I think now we tell someone."

It was the right thing to do, Madeleine thought. But her heart sunk. Admitting she had broken curfew meant the end of her scholarship. And maybe worse, the end of her new friendships. But somebody could get hurt. and that somebody could be one of the very friends she was afraid of losing.

"Let's go," she said.

***

Madeleine had never been inside Madame Puant's office, and she was amazed by the sheer grandness of the whole place. Red velvety carpet blanketed the floor, like the hallway's, only nicer, and Madame's desk was made of a dark, ornately carved wood. Madeleine could see cherubs and trees and nymphs . . .

But all of that fled from her mind as Ophelia began to explain why they'd all come.

Goodbye, Dario Quincy Academy . . ., Madeleine thought.

She looked at the ground while Ophelia finished. The quiet seemed to stretch for minutes. Madeleine started fidgeting. She just wished Madame would expel them and be done with it. And, of course, get rid of the cult.

Finally, Madame Puant said, "So, let me get this straight. The five of you found some secret tunnels under the school. And then found a room where a circle of hooded figures stood chanting around an altar—an altar filled with *your* stolen trinkets—and then they chased you down a stone tunnel? And today you all had nosebleeds at the exact same time, and five bloody children's dolls appeared on your dressing table? Is this what you're telling me? Ophelia?"

When Madame said it like that, it sounded ridiculous, Madeleine thought. She could hear the doubt in Ophelia's voice too: "I know it sounds crazy, Madame, but . . ."

Madame cut her off with a wave of her hand. "It doesn't sound crazy, Ophelia."

Madeleine found the strength to look up. Maybe Madame did believe them, after all.

Madame went on, "It sounds like a desperate ploy to either get attention or to get out of class or the hysterical rantings of five girls who talked themselves into something ridiculous." She trained her eyes on Madeleine. "I thought you'd be better than this, Madeleine. You are an exemplary student and this ... well, this is just absurd."

Madeleine's face turned hot with shame. But it quickly cooled as she asked herself, what about the dolls?

"Madame," she said excitedly, "We have proof. You mentioned it yourself—the dolls! Come look!"

The girls all nodded excitedly.

"Very well," Madame said. "Let's have a look at these dolls. Though I'm inclined to believe you constructed them yourself too. But—I'll humor you."

Madeleine felt excitement rippling in her stomach as they walked to Ophelia's room. Earlier, she had wanted nothing more than to *not* tell Madame. Now, she was desperate for Madame to believe them.

Ophelia opened her door with a flourish. Only a "ta-da!" was missing. For a second, Madeleine had to fight the urge to giggle.

But when they stepped into the room, there was no reason to laugh. The dolls were gone.

Madeleine's jaw dropped. "Madame, I *swear* they were here!"

Madame glared at each girl in turn. "You have wasted my time and the time of this academy. You are banned from class for the rest of the week. Maybe you can use that time to think about the ramifications of making up stories!"

She turned on her heel to exit, and Ophelia said to her retreating back, "Wait! We'll show you tonight! At midnight!" But Madame disappeared before Ophelia could finish.

Ophelia slumped on her bed and put her head in her hands. The other girls flopped on the floor.

Madeleine was shocked—they couldn't go to class for a whole week. A day hadn't gone by where she hadn't been in a studio since she was three years old. Not one day. Even when she'd gotten an injury, she'd gone to the studio to watch the others.

Even so, Madeleine was relieved. They hadn't been kicked out.

"You guys, this sucks," she said. "But—we didn't get kicked out."

Kayley, Sophie, and Emma nodded their heads. Ophelia continued to stare at the dressing table. Finally, she spoke. "Listen, I *know* what we saw. We just need proof, that's all."

Sophie looked up glumly. "How are we going to do that? Why didn't we take the dolls with us? That was so dumb."

Ophelia nodded. "It was dumb. And it was dumb not to take pictures or video last night. Which is why we're going back tonight."

Chapter 13

Kayley crossed and uncrossed her arms. "No. Way."

Ophelia grabbed Kayley's shoulders. "Think about it. This is the only way to prove to Madame Puant what's happening! And I don't know about you, but I don't want some freakish cult trying to kill us in our sleep. And don't you want your grandma's gloves back?"

Kayley looked away. Madeleine knew that Ophelia had won.

"Yes. We have to go back tonight," Emma said.

Everyone looked at her. She shrugged. "Look, I was freaked out last night, but now I'm just mad. Ophelia's right. We need to end this thing, whatever it is. And this time, we come with cameras."

"OK," Sophie said. "But don't you think they'll be expecting us this time?"

"That's a good point," Ophelia said.

Madeleine sat up. "The prop room."

Kayley stared at her. "Yeah, the prop room. What about it?"

"Wouldn't there be cloaks? Or *something* in there we could use?" Madeleine asked.

Ophelia sat up too. "Yes! Last year we put on a ballet that had, like, a million grim reapers." Madeleine scrunched her face up. "Don't ask," Ophelia continued. "Anyway, I know exactly where they are. Brilliant, Madeleine! Maybe that's where they got their cloaks . . ."

Madeleine felt the glow from before. Never at her old school did she have friends like this.

Emma said, "I bet I know where the cloaks

are too. Sophie and I will grab five now, and at midnight, we'll go down to the tunnels and bust those suckers."

Sophie gawked at Emma and Emma shrugged. "No one is looking to go into the prop room today. Besides, we're banned from class—what else are we going to do?"

Sophie gave a slow smile and said, "Beats sitting in our rooms for three hours."

Kayley said, "Well, if the wonder twins are in, I guess I am too."

"Me too," Madeleine said.

Ophelia grinned. "Damn straight you are."

***

Dressed in cloaks that shaded their faces, the five of them stood outside the tunnel doors and took deep breaths.

Getting to the tunnels hadn't been easy. Hall monitors were patrolling the halls more frequently than they had the night before. Madeleine didn't think that was a coincidence. But the girls made it to the dank and musty tunnels without incident. As they stood in front of the medieval-looking door, each of them grabbed another girl's hand in what had become their sneaking-around formation. And then Ophelia turned the knob.

Madeleine cringed while the door creaked open. She really, really hoped this plan would work.

When they stepped out to the hall, no one else was there, but candles flickered in their holders. The hooded figures were around somewhere. Madeleine knew it. Now the girls just had to sneak up to the room and film them.

Easy peasy.

Madeleine's hands started to shake. She felt a cold sweat break out over her body. The image of the hooded figures chasing her kept flashing in her mind.

Ophelia whispered, "Let's go."

They clustered together and began to tiptoe down the dark hall.

When they reached the branch of the tunnel they'd gone to before, they heard no chanting.

"This was it, wasn't it?" Ophelia asked quietly.

A deep male voice behind them said loudly, "Yes, this was it. Why don't you come join our party, girls?"

Fear shot through Madeleine. She turned and tried to run but a wall of hooded figures surrounded them on every side, blocking any exit, all wearing some sort of black mask, plastic or latex. The masks had blank eyes and downturned mouths. She saw something glint in the candlelight, slender and silver, in one of the figures' hands and knew it was a knife. Her knees threatened to give out.

"Please don't hurt us," she said.

The man said gruffly, "You've come to a place you have no business coming to. And you've almost ruined our work." The hooded figures in his line advanced on the girls slowly until the only path left led into the room with the artifacts.

The girls all huddled close together, shaking.

Ophelia cleared her throat, "Please, sir—"

"Silence!" the man roared. "You are in a sacred space, and you will not speak unless spoken to. Though you have trespassed, you can be of use to us. We are here to help you—you must know that—even though you are ungrateful."

Madeleine furrowed her eyebrows. Help them? This didn't feel very helpful to her.

A smaller robed figure came forward—the one holding a knife. "And you can help *us* . . . by giving up your blood."

Shadowy hands grabbed each girl and held their arms back. As Madeleine saw the blade come toward her, a scream ripped through her throat.

"It will be over quickly. Don't worry," said the man who'd been doing all the talking. Madeleine turned to the other girls, sharing with them a last look of terror.

Madeleine was first in line. One of the masked figures picked up her necklace from the altar and brought it toward her. For a moment, she thought they might just put it around her neck. Instead, the person gripping Madeleine thrust out Madeleine's arm.

"Spill the blood on the necklace," the deep-voiced man said.

The rest of the figures started to chant in the strange unknown language, and the person holding the necklace dangled it underneath Madeleine's forearm.

The knife got closer and closer until Madeleine felt its blade press against her wrist. She waited to pass out, but something kept her wide awake.

The voices of Ophelia, Kayley, Emma, and Sophie traveled over to her, all yelling, but they sounded far away, as if they were on a different planet. The tip of the knife pressed slowly down as pain shot through Madeleine's arm. She could hear her voice turn into a scream.

And then she heard another voice. The most beautiful voice she'd ever heard.

"Stop this at once."

Madame Puant slammed her cane on the cement floor. Behind her stood at least five faculty members and six police officers.

The person holding Madeleine let go, and she fell to the floor. The other girls were released too, and they rushed to her, wrapping Madeleine in a hug.

"Just what is the meaning of this? You think you can come to *my* school and menace *my* girls? You are sorely mistaken!"

Chapter 14

The police officers stormed up to the hooded figures, handcuffing each one. No one seemed to put up a fight.

The lead man's big booming voice began to quiver: "Don't hurt anyone here. We were just trying to help."

Madame Puant strode over to him and yanked off his mask. Madeleine threw her hands up to her mouth. Staring in wonder, she said, "Mr. Barnes?"

Her heart sank. How could it be Mr. Barnes?

One by one, more masks were taken off. Madame Puant looked livid. The person who had held the knife was Ms. Jamison. Other teachers Madeleine had seen around the halls were also in the mix.

Madame Puant stuttered, dumbstruck. "Wha . . . ? Why would you . . . ?"

Mr. Barnes, his hair and eyes wild, began to plead with Madame. "Please, Betsy, you don't understand. We were trying to save these girls."

Madame Puant pounded her cane on the ground. "By killing them? By stabbing them with a knife?"

Madeleine shrank from the power in Madame's voice. As petite as she was, Madame Puant was no one to be messed with. Madeleine hoped she would never be at the end of that yell. Right then, though, there was no one in the world she'd rather have had by her side.

Mr. Barnes flinched but continued to beg: "We weren't going to kill them, Betsy. Don't be absurd! We needed their blood for the tokens we took to ward off the bad energy, the curses that plague this academy! That's what we've been doing here. These girls, your other students—they should be grateful! Once they gifted us with their presence, we *knew* the fates had smiled upon us. Their blood would have sealed off the school from evil, protected it!"

Madame Puant shook her head in disbelief. "I'm the one being absurd?"

"Betsy, you know as well as we do that this school is malevolent," Ms. Jamison said. "There is something not right about this place—I'm positive it's haunted, cursed. And you know as well as I do that the best dancers are those who get harmed! What about *Giselle*? The dancers who have die—"

"Nonsense!" Madame Puant said. "The only curse on this house is the curse of you crazy people. Officers, please escort these lunatics out of here."

She turned to walk out, then turned back again. "And you will kindly address me as Madame Puant from now on. Rest assured, I will make sure you never work in this state again. Or any other state in which I can wield my influence."

The officers took the hooded figures away, leaving the girls in the room alone. Tears coursed down Madeleine's face as she slid out of their group hug. When they stepped back, she saw she wasn't the only one crying. She took a deep breath, bent down, and picked up her necklace.

"It's about time I got this back," she said.

Ophelia grinned and grabbed her ring from the altar, sliding it onto her finger. "I told you I didn't steal it."

"True. But you did just involve me in a cult ritual where someone almost sliced me with a knife."

Ophelia laughed. "*So* picky. Anyway, you heard him. He picked the tokens from the best dancers. That includes you. Any more finger pointing and I'll start taking credit for your ballet skills too."

She grinned at Madeleine, and Madeleine grinned back. "Why didn't I bring candy?" Kayley said.

A contorted shadow dashed along the wall.

The girls shrieked and jumped.

"Come on, girls," Madame Puant said, twisting her head in from around the corner. "Let's get you out of these tunnels. I think you may have earned some ice cream. In the infirmary, though, so we can make sure you are OK."

The five girls linked hands and followed Madame Puant to the stairs and out of the creepy tunnels.

Chapter 15

"I still don't get it," Sophie said through a great big slurp of ice cream. "What were they doing down there? And how did we all get nosebleeds at the same time?"

Nurse John fluttered back and forth among the girls, checking vital signs and ice-cream levels. When he came to check Madeleine's pulse, she thought it might be twice as high as it should be. Not because she'd almost been killed but because he was so good looking.

He smiled at her. "Perfect vitals."

Madeleine had to remember to close her mouth. She wondered how much ice cream he saw in there. She tried to swallow her scoop with dignity.

Ophelia huffed. "Sophie, weren't you paying attention? We're the best dancers—of course the crazy hooded freaks would target us for whatever stupid ritual they had planned."

Kayley happily took a bite of her ice cream. "Yeah. You know. The usual."

Emma sighed. "Well, whatever that was, I'm glad it's over. Although . . ."

"Although, what?" Madeleine said.

"There's that thing about *Giselle* . . ."

Ophelia shot Emma a look and said, "We don't need to make Madeleine paranoid. She just got here, and we want her to stay around."

Ophelia smiled at Madeleine. The warm feeling that Madeleine had felt before spread through her again. This was what it was like to be a part of something. She smiled back. And although she was dying to hear about the whole *Giselle* thing, she decided she'd savor the moment now and ask later.

"But what about the nosebleeds?" Sophie said.

Ophelia slammed down her ice-cream bowl. "Sophie, don't you listen to anything?"

Emma piped up: "Oh, come on, Ophelia. It still doesn't make sense to me either."

"It's like how Nurse John explained it to Madame Puant," Madeleine said. "Evidently, there's some chemical in the tunnels that causes nosebleeds. Remember how tweaked out Mr. Barnes looked all the time? The place is toxic. The staff is doing a major clean down there. Then I think she'd going to cement those tunnels off."

"I think the real question is, why were those tunnels created anyway?" Kayley asked.

No one had an answer. After a minute, Sophie said, "So, I'm sorry, but about the nosebleeds . . ."

Ophelia threw her head back and groaned, along with Kayley. Even Emma looked impatient.

"No, I get *how* we got them and what caused

them," Sophie continued. "But why did we all get them at exactly the same time?"

The room got quiet. Uneasily, Ophelia said, "Maybe the toxicity hit us all at the same time?" But even she didn't look convinced.

Madeleine took a deep breath and decided to plunge in. These were her friends after all, and friends could say anything to each other. "Guys, I don't want to sound crazy, but I think those hooded freaks were right. There is something off about this place. I mean, they went about everything all wrong, but . . . I felt it the first minute I walked up the outside steps. Dario Quincy Academy *is* strange. And maybe even evil. Am I the only one who feels it too?"

One by one, each of them shook their heads.

"I feel it," Sophie said.

"Me too," said Emma.

Kayley pointed her ice-cream spoon at her and said, "Pretty perceptive, newbie. Yeah, something's not right."

Ophelia's lips were a thin line. "Yeah, Madeleine. Dario Quincy Academy is the best ballet school in the world. But something isn't right here. Something is very wrong. And I don't think closing up the tunnels will help, no matter what the reason they were built in the first place."

Madeleine shivered.

At that moment, Madame Puant stepped in the room. "All right, enough ice cream. You all have ballet class in the morning, so you need some sleep."

The clock read *2:00 A.M.*, and Madeleine was tired. And then she realized what Madame said.

"Wait, we get to go to class?" She looked excitedly at the other girls, who had the same looks on their faces.

"Well, it would hardly do to have our school's star investigators banished from ballet."

All five of them whooped. Madame looked the girls in the eye, one by one. "But if you ladies break curfew again, I won't be so nice. This is a big house . . . and very unique. I would hate it if something happened to you girls." A dark cloud passed over her expression. "Strange things can happen to people late at night. Especially in this house. Now good night, girls. See you in the morning."

As Madame walked out the door, Madeleine began to think about her new life and her new school. She touched her necklace—on her neck where it was supposed to be, finally. She looked around at her new friends. Maybe there was something wrong at Dario Quincy. But with her family behind her and her friends in front of her and ballet all around her, Madeleine could think of no other place she'd rather be.

THE DARIO QUINCY ACADEMY OF DANCE

Ballet. Gossip. Evil Spirits.

SEEK THE TRUTH

AND FIND THE CAUSE

WITH

THE PARANORMALISTS

THE HAUNTING OF
APARTMENT 101
MEGAN ATWOOD

THE TERROR OF
BLACK EAGLE TAVERN
MEGAN ATWOOD

THE MAYHEM ON
MOHAWK AVENUE
MEGAN ATWOOD

THE BRIDGE OF
DEATH
MEGAN ATWOOD

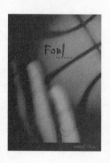

AFTER THE DUST SETTLED

The world is over.
Can you survive what's next?

About the Author

Megan Atwood is the author of more than fourteen books for children and young adults and is a college teacher who teaches all kinds of writing. She clearly has the best job in the world. She lives in Minneapolis, Minnesota, with two cats, a boy, and probably a couple of ghosts.